DO NOT LET THIS BOOK FALL INTO ENEMY HANDS!

AGENT HANDBOOK:

How to Foil Your Enemies, Double-Cross Your Friends, And Find the Clues First

SCHOLASTIC INC.

NEW YORK TORONTO LONDON AUCKLAND
SYDNEY MEXICO CITY NEW DELHI HONG KONG

Library of Congress Control Number: 2010920561

ISBN: 978-1-4351-2583-4

10 9 8 7 6 5 4 3 2 1   10 11 12 13 14

First edition, May 2010

Printed in the USA   23

Scholastic US: 557 Broadway • New York, NY 10012
Scholastic Canada: 604 King Street West • Toronto, ON M5V 1E1
Scholastic New Zealand Limited: Private Bag 94407 • Greenmount, Manukau 2141
Scholastic UK Ltd.: Euston House • 24 Eversholt Street • London NW1 1DB

Memorandum

To: All Cahill Agents
From: William McIntyre
Regarding: The hunt for the 39 Clues

Dear Agent:

If you are holding this handbook, it means you have been chosen for a hunt of vital importance – both to the Cahill family and the world at large. You are a member of the Cahill family, the most powerful family ever to walk the earth. The secret of the Cahill power has been lost, and only by assembling 39 Clues hidden around the world can it be found again. This is your challenge . . . and your burden.

I do not exaggerate when I tell you that the Cahills have shaped human history. The world's most famous leaders, explorers, inventors, and artists were all members of your family. But if the Cahills are the most talented people, they are also some of the most ruthless. And you are competing directly against them in the Clue hunt.

This handbook contains the most up-to-date information we have about the Cahill family and the Clue hunt. Many agents sacrificed their lives to bring you the data contained inside. I hope this handbook will help you in the dark days to come.

Good luck. You're going to need it.

William McIntyre

Want to beat the competition? Then you better know who you're up against. The Cahill family is made up of four warring branches formed when the family split apart 500 years ago. Each branch has special skills in hunting Clues . . . and eliminating rivals.

Founded by Luke Cahill, the Lucians are master strategists, the best code breakers, and the sneakiest branch of the Cahill family. They're also the wealthiest – the filthiest of the world's most filthy rich. But power is what really drives the Lucian branch, which is why the vast majority of world leaders come from the Lucian families. The US diplomatic corps, for instance, is riddled with Lucian agents. Born with a sense of how to get and use power, Lucians also know how to keep enemies under control. If fear and intimidation don't work, Lucians turn to poison. If you are going up against a Lucian operative, make sure you have a medical kit full of antidotes at the ready. You'll never know when you might need it.

The brilliant Katherine Cahill was the founder of the Ekaterina branch. Her descendants are geniuses – out-of-the-box thinkers who dream up new medicines, ultra-fast computers, and designs for space shuttles. Their curiosity is endless, and they are fascinated by the technology of ancient cultures. Along with the world's top doctors, scientists, and inventors, the Ekaterina branch has a healthy share of archaeologists. But while Ekaterinas are focused thinkers, they make plenty of time for Clue hunting, too. Their wealth of gadgetry and relentless logic have taken them far in the Clue hunt. Never try to outthink an Ekat. You'll end up with a lot worse than a headache.

Thomas Cahill was one of the younger Cahill siblings, but he was by far the largest and the strongest. And the family branch he founded is just the same. The Tomas have won more athletic contests, competitions, and meets than any of the other branches combined. Their amazing feats of endurance and courage make the Tomas some of the world's most famous explorers. If there's an ocean to be crossed or a mountain to be climbed, the Tomas heart and staggering strength get the job done. This branch has formidable Clue hunters, so stay alert. And remember, if you're racing against Tomas agents for a Clue, don't bother. They will always outdistance you.

Jane Cahill was the youngest of the four Cahill siblings, still just a child when the family split. But don't make the mistake of underestimating Jane's descendants on the Clue hunt. As the world's most famous musicians, painters, writers, and artists, the Janus use their immense creative energy to sneak their way around formidable obstacles. The Janus own Hollywood. They dominate the box office, the Academy Awards, and top music charts around the world. With legions of fans at the ready, the Janus have a worldwide network in place and are always able to pounce. If you're going head-to-head with a Janus, keep your eyes open. This branch has also mastered the art of disguise.

Some claim they are renegades from the four family branches, some claim they are a branch on their own, and some claim they are outsiders. There is very little concrete information available about the Madrigals, except that they seem to know more than anybody about the Clue hunt. Madrigals are very dangerous. **Avoid them at all costs....**

Known Strongholds: Around the Globe

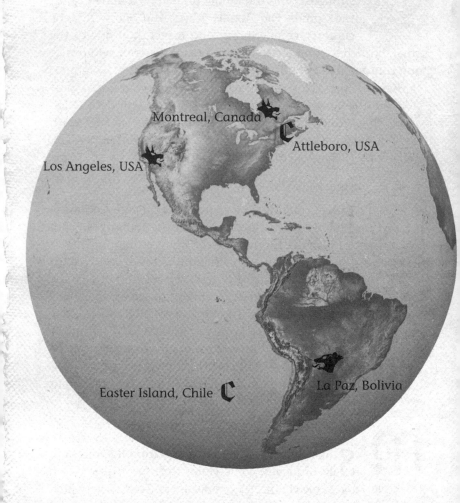

Montreal, Canada

Attleboro, USA

Los Angeles, USA

Easter Island, Chile

La Paz, Bolivia

Western Hemisphere

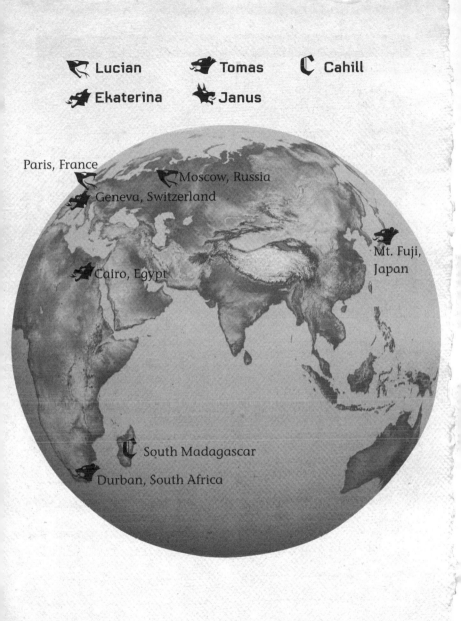

Lucian
Tomas
Cahill
Ekaterina
Janus

Paris, France
Moscow, Russia
Geneva, Switzerland
Mt. Fuji, Japan
Cairo, Egypt
South Madagascar
Durban, South Africa

Eastern Hemisphere

LUCIAN

continued

EKATERINA

JANUS

TOMAS

ℳ

IMPORTANT STATS

AGENT NAME: GRACE MADELEINE CAHILL

FAMILY BRANCH: UNKNOWN

STATUS: HIGH

HOMETOWN: ATTLEBORO, USA

INTERESTS: AVIATION, CARTOGRAPHY, ANTHROPOLOGY, CHEMISTRY, EGYPTIAN MAUs

SKILLS: STUNT FLYING, FORGERY, MANIPULATION, LOCK PICKING, CHARMING SECURITY GUARDS, ERASING HER FOOTSTEPS

CLUE-HUNTING STRENGTHS: PRIVATE PLANES, VAST NETWORK OF CONTACTS AROUND THE WORLD, ADVANCED SURVEILLANCE TECHNOLOGY

WEAKNESS: OBSESSION WITH SECRECY MAKES IT DIFFICULT FOR PEOPLE TO TRUST HER

AGENT FILE: CAHILL, G.

Notes

Grace spent her entire life searching for the 39 Clues. As a child, she accompanied her father on secret trips. After college, she struck out on her own, disappearing for months at a time as she explored remote areas of the world in her plane, *The Flying Lemur.* Grace continued this tradition with her own daughter, Hope, who grew up studying the secrets of the Cahills and the 39 Clues. However, Hope's Clue hunt came to a tragic end in a fire that killed both her and her husband. In the wake of this loss, Grace focused her energy on arranging an official competition to find the Clues. Some were surprised that she included Amy and Dan, wondering why she'd send her orphaned grandchildren into danger, considering the fate that befell their parents. Did Grace have one final trick up her sleeve? Or did she decide that assembling the 39 Clues was worth *any* sacrifice—including two more of her family's lives?

Codicil to the Last Will and Testament of Grace Cahill

I, Grace Cahill, a resident of Massachusetts, being of sound mind, declare this to be a valid codicil to my Last Will and Testament.

Fellow Cahills, the fact that you are reading this document means I am dead. Some of you may think good riddance! I have made many enemies in my life, and few friends.

My relatives, you know by now that you belong to the Cahill family, but few of you realize just how important our family is. I tell you the Cahills have had a greater impact on human civilization than any other family in history.

You stand on the brink of our greatest challenge. Each of you has the potential to succeed, but only one of you will. Your challenge is to find 39 Clues hidden around the world that lead to the lost secret of the Cahill family power.

Although I have lied many times in my life—for good reasons and for bad—I will not lie to you now. The hunt for the Clues will not be easy. But the reward is beyond measure—the most important treasure in the world.

You will not get much help in your search. Know that hints are everywhere, and nothing is quite what it seems. And know that I have faith in you. After all, you hold the fate of the world in your hands.

Grace Cahill

Signed: Grace Cahill

William McIntyre, esq.

Witnessed: William McIntyre, esq.

Date: August 18, 2008

GRACE MADELEINE CAHILL

1929 – 2008

The world joins the residents of Attleboro in mourning the loss of Grace Cahill. She was known for her generosity, intelligence, and strong personality.

Cahill was born in 1929 to Edith and James Cahill. She attended some of New England's most famous schools along with her siblings, Beatrice and Fiske. Even at a young age, Grace Cahill was known for speaking her mind. Her teachers always appreciated her participation in class.

Cahill attended Radcliffe College (now a part of Harvard University). She studied anthropology and chemistry. Cahill became famous on campus for her daring chemistry experiments. In honor of her achievements, Cahill's parents donated the Grace Cahill Chemistry Laboratory to the college. Its fireproof walls still stand today.

After graduating in 1950, Cahill traveled around the world studying communities in Africa and Asia. The villages she lived in were so remote that Grace was out of contact with her family for years. She always

PHOTO ARCHIVE

reappeared, however, and became famous for her anthropology articles. During her travels, Cahill also became a skilled mapmaker. She flew her own single-engine plane, which allowed her to explore previously uncharted areas.

In 1959, Cahill married Nathaniel Hartford. Their daughter, Hope, was born in 1960. Two years later, Cahill's younger brother, Fiske, mysteriously disappeared. The cause of his disappearance is unknown and Fiske is now presumed dead. This tragedy was followed by the sudden death of Hartford in 1967, of unknown causes while on a business trip in Moscow. Although heartbroken by these losses, Cahill continued her research and conducted chemistry experiments in her private laboratory. She also frequently invited scientists, artists, and diplomats from around the world to visit her in Attleboro.

In 2001, Hope Cahill and her husband, Arthur Trent, were tragically killed in a fire that broke out in their Boston home. Cahill is survived by her elder sister, Beatrice, her grandchildren, Amy and Dan Cahill, and numerous distant cousins.

That's one way of saying it.

destroying anyone who disagreed with her

The school made them replace the lab Grace burned down

seem fishy to anyone else?

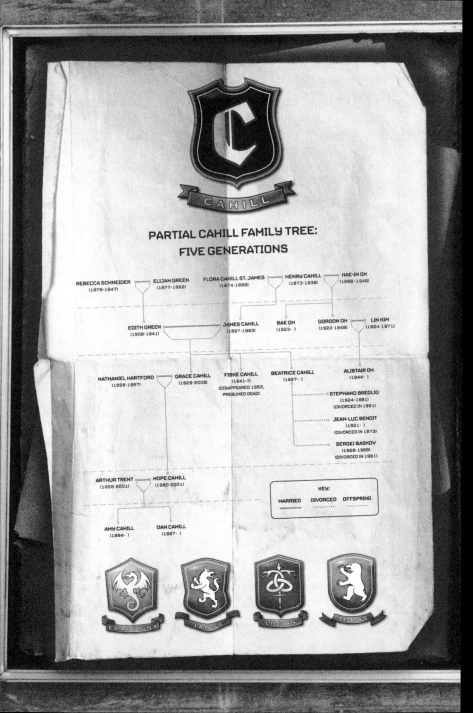

YOUR FAMILY TREE:

TOP SECRET

IMPORTANT STATS

AGENT NAME: DAN CAHILL

FAMILY BRANCH: UNKNOWN

STATUS: HIGH; SON OF HOPE CAHILL

HOMETOWN: BOSTON, USA

AGE: 11

INTERESTS: BASEBALL CARDS, GRAVE RUBBINGS, VIDEO GAMES, BECOMING A NINJA

SKILLS: MATH, PUZZLES, PHOTOGRAPHIC MEMORY, ANNOYING HIS SISTER

CLUE-HUNTING STRENGTHS: HAS NO IDEA HOW DANGEROUS THE HUNT WILL BE

WEAKNESS: HAS NO IDEA HOW DANGEROUS THE HUNT WILL BE

Notes

As expected, Dan views the hunt for the 39 Clues as a big adventure. He enjoys breaking into moldy tombs, avoiding explosions, and escaping ninja attacks. Above all, though, Dan appreciates the chance to feel his parents come alive for him. He was only four when they died, but our spies report that Dan feels close to his parents as he continues the hunt they weren't able to complete. However, there are dangerous secrets about Hope and Arthur that Grace never shared, and they won't remain hidden forever. It is unclear what will happen when Dan discovers the truth. Will he continue the hunt, or will the shock be too much to handle? We fear Dan will prefer his old memories of his parents— distant, perfect, and incapable of betrayal.

Dan's Favorite
Clue-hunting
companion, Saladin

TOP SECRET

IMPORTANT STATS

AGENT NAME: AMY CAHILL

FAMILY BRANCH: UNKNOWN

STATUS: HIGH; DAUGHTER OF HOPE CAHILL

HOMETOWN: BOSTON, USA

AGE: 14

INTERESTS: HISTORY, BAKING, ICE SKATING, LIBRARIES

SKILLS: PROBLEM-SOLVING, RESEARCH, ESCAPING NEAR-DEATH SITUATIONS

CLUE-HUNTING STRENGTHS: REMARKABLE GRASP OF HISTORY AND GEOGRAPHY

WEAKNESS: SEVERE SHYNESS, FEAR OF CROWDS

AGENT FILE: CAHILL, A.

Notes

We've been observing Amy for many years. She has no idea that she's been preparing to find the 39 Clues her entire life, but the time she spent with her grandmother reading history, studying maps, and solving puzzles was actually part of a carefully planned training regime. Grace reported Amy's activities on a regular basis and was pleased with her progress. Her only real concern was about Amy's shyness; Grace hoped that the competition wouldn't start until Amy was older and more confident. However, the plans changed, and Grace had to send her grandchildren on the hunt before their training was complete. Although she feared for their safety, Grace had no choice. We had to continue, or our entire mission would fail. All we can do now is wait and watch.

Dear Madame Cahill,

As you requested, I set up a little "test" for Amy. You were right. It's time we began evaluating the children for their strengths and weaknesses.

I arranged for Amy to become separated from her class during a field trip to the Museum of Fine Arts. An actress I hired distracted Amy by pretending to be an old woman in distress. By the time Amy had finished helping her, the class had disappeared. She was alone in the Art of the Ancient World gallery. I monitored the situation through the museum's security cameras.

Amy knew that her class had been heading off to see the Renoir painting *Dance at Bougival*, but there was no one to ask for directions. I had spoken with the museum director and made sure that there would be no security guards to assist her.

Amy stayed calm when she realized her class was gone. She pulled out a map of the museum, but when she looked at it, she grimaced. The map was organized by time periods, which meant she had to figure out when Renoir lived. I heard her muttering:

"Renoir — okay, that sounds French. French paintings, um . . . I don't know . . . Wait! I've seen a Renoir! It's at Grace's house — and it's next to . . . what? I think . . . it's a Monet. Do I know anything about Monet? Um . . . his artwork isn't completely realistic? Oh! Grace says that he painted impressions! And impression paintings were popular . . . in . . . the 1800s. Yay! Nineteenth Century!"

Then I had the lights in the gallery shut off. I heard Amy gasp. The gallery looked frightening in the dark with all those headless statues. I could see the outlines of Amy's hands shaking as she held on to the map. However, she stayed focused and crept against the wall until she found the exit and ran to meet up with her class.

I was impressed with Amy and believe she shows promise. However, there is still much for her to learn. I recommend that we arrange many more of these tests. We should start evaluating Dan as well.

Sincerely,

William McIntyre, esq.

TRACE AMY AND DAN'S JOURNEY

START
Attleboro, MA
USA

B

TOP SECRET

IMPORTANT STATS

AGENT NAME: HOPE CAHILL

FAMILY BRANCH: UNKNOWN

STATUS: HIGH; DAUGHTER OF GRACE CAHILL

HOMETOWN: ATTLEBORO, USA

INTERESTS: ARCHAEOLOGY, BAKING, SINGING, EXPLOSIVES

SKILLS: PUZZLES, CODE BREAKING, DISGUISES, HIDING SECRET ITEMS

Notes

Growing up, Hope was the golden child of the Cahill family. Even her crafty uncle Alistair Oh was charmed by the young Hope's liveliness and warmth. However, as she grew older, we watched Hope become secretive and reserved. At first, evidence suggested that Hope was simply taking the Clue hunt more seriously. However, our spies reported a more disturbing theory. There were rumors that Hope and her husband, Arthur, were working on a dangerous scheme that threatened the entire family. When Hope and Arthur were killed in a fire, some Cahills were heartbroken, but many were relieved. Investigation into this matter is ongoing.

BOSTON GENERAL HOSPITAL

Date: January 3, 1999

Patient name: Hope Cahill

Age: 39

Sex: Female

Reason for visit: Sprained wrist

Procedures: X-ray

Comments: The patient was brought to the hospital against her will after a minor car accident. When I told her we would need to X-ray her wrist, she became visibly anxious. I assured her that the procedure was completely painless, but she was distressed and tried to leave. Her husband convinced the patient to stay, saying, "Don't worry, it will mean nothing to him."

When the X-ray technician finished, I reviewed the films. The patient's wrist was fine, but to my amazement, there seemed to be a strange object in her arm. It looked like some sort of electronic chip. I was concerned and tried to discuss the matter with the patient, but she was silent. I suspected Mafia involvement but chose not to alert the police.

IMPORTANT STATS

AGENT NAME: ARTHUR TRENT

FAMILY BRANCH: UNKNOWN

STATUS: HIGH; GRACE CAHILL'S SON-IN-LAW

HOMETOWN: BOSTON, USA

INTERESTS: FAMILY, JAZZ, MEXICAN FOOD, TRAVEL, NINJAS

SKILLS: MATH, PHYSICS, TEACHING, HIDING HIS PAST

Notes

Arthur Trent's life changed when he married Hope Cahill. He became her partner in the Clue hunt and a committed father to his two children. However, recent intelligence suggests that Arthur may not have been entirely what he seemed. There is evidence that he had known about the Cahills for years. It is not a coincidence that Arthur and Hope met in Turkey—Arthur accepted the teaching post because he knew that Grace Cahill's daughter was working there. We are investigating why our screening process failed and, more important, what Arthur did with the Cahill secrets he uncovered.

TOP SECRET

CAHILL

IMPORTANT STATS

AGENT NAME: WILLIAM MCINTYRE

FAMILY BRANCH: UNKNOWN

STATUS: LOW; WORKS FOR GRACE CAHILL

HOMETOWN: BOSTON, USA

OCCUPATION: LAWYER/FORMER NAVY SEAL

SKILLS: SECRECY, STEALTH, CONCEALMENT, ESPIONAGE

Notes

William McIntyre was Grace Cahill's longtime friend, lawyer, and confidant. However, there are rumors that he's not entirely what he seems. Cahills on the hunt have spotted William in odd, Clue-related locations around the world. Some swear they've seen him meeting with a mysterious man in black. Questions about William' loyalty abound. Is he simply carrying out Grace's wishes by organizing the hunt for the 39 Clues? Or does the enigmatic lawyer have his own agenda? His actions are certainly suspicious, but there's insufficient evidence to support the worst of the rumors—that William is secretly working for the Madrigals.

No 16463

Registry of Vital Records and Statistics
CERTIFICATE OF BIRTH

This is to certify that _William Gideon McIntyre_

Mother's name: _Winifred Cahill Green_

Father's name: _Edward Bernard McIntyre_

Sex _male_ was born on _May 3, 1959_

according to Birth Record No. _16463_

filed in the _Dorchester_

Office of this Bureau on_____

Right foot

assorted
letterhead
(for forging Cahill letters)

OFFICIAL · CAHILL · CORRESPONDENCE

------------------------------ FOLD ------------------------------

------------------------------ FOLD ------------------------------

OFFICIAL · CAHILL · CORRESPONDENCE

- FOLD -

- FOLD -

OFFICIAL · CAHILL · CORRESPONDENCE

FOLD

FOLD

PLACE STAMP

FOLD

FOLD

- FOLD -

- FOLD -

- F O L D -

- F O L D -

- FOLD -

- FOLD -

Spring on dad

www. the 39 clues.com

LUCIAN

Lucian Branch

Current Branch Leaders: Isabel and Vikram Kabra

Known Strongholds: Paris, France and Moscow, Russia

Founder: Luke Cahill

Famous Lucians: Napoleon Bonaparte, Ben Franklin, Winston Churchill

Characteristics: All of the greatest world leaders come from the Lucian branch – the presidents, generals, and diplomats who brought peace and prosperity to their people. But Lucians are also schemers, plotters, and strategists – the type of people who start wars in the first place. Don't turn your back on the Lucians – they may just put their daggers in it.

Intelligence Report: Their utter ruthlessness and their obsession with world domination make the Lucians extremely dangerous competitors on the hunt for the 39 Clues. They see all the angles and exploit any weaknesses in other teams. The Lucians will do anything – including lying, stealing, and assassinating – in order to get to the Clues first. They came closest to collecting all the Clues in Russia at the turn of this century. If it wasn't for a Madrigal intervention, we might all be living under Lucian rule today.

Lucian Stronghold
Location:

Moscow

IMPORTANT STATS

AGENT NAME: LUKE CAHILL

FAMILY BRANCH: LUCIAN

STATUS: FOUNDER

HOMETOWN: IRELAND

SKILLS: LEADERSHIP, MANIPULATION, INTELLIGENCE, SECRECY

SYMBOL: A SNAKE

PRIZED POSSESSION: A DAGGER

FAMOUS DESCENDANTS: ISAAC NEWTON, NAPOLEON BONAPARTE, CATHERINE THE GREAT, WINSTON CHURCHILL, BENJAMIN FRANKLIN

AGENT FILE: CAHILL, L.

Notes

The eldest of Gideon Cahill's four children, Luke felt that he was entitled to know all his father's secrets. He was furious when he discovered his father's plan to divide the Clues among the siblings. Luke's rage drove him to break into Gideon's laboratory with the aim of discovering the remaining Clues. The rest of the story varies dramatically, depending on the source. By some accounts, Thomas, Jane, and Katherine saw Luke sneaking around right before the fire started and blamed their brother for Gideon's death.

Lucians maintain that Luke was simply in the wrong place at the wrong time. Either way, it is accepted that Luke left Ireland after the fire, enraged by Thomas and Katherine's accusations, and hurt that his favorite sister, Jane, seemed to believe them. Luke traveled to England, where he became a close advisor to Henry VIII and started a long tradition of Lucians in politics. Is the Lucian reputation for deception a myth? Or is it rooted in a legacy of lies, trickery . . . and murder?

AGENT FILE: SPASKY, I.

TOP SECRET

IMPORTANT STATS

AGENT NAME: IRINA SPASKY

FAMILY BRANCH: LUCIAN

STATUS: HIGH; REPORTS DIRECTLY TO ISABEL AND VIKRAM KABRA

HOMETOWN: ST. PETERSBURG, RUSSIA

INTERESTS: POISON DELIVERY MECHANISMS, POLE-VAULTING

SKILLS: EXPLOSIVES, ESPIONAGE, SECRET ASSASSINATIONS

CLUE-HUNTING STRENGTHS: THE YOUNGEST KGB AGENT IN HISTORY, IRINA IS ONE OF THE MOST TALENTED SPIES IN THE WORLD

WEAKNESS: A DEATH IN THE FAMILY CHANGED HER TACTICS

Notes

Irina Spasky is a highly accomplished (and feared) Lucian. She single-handedly collected more Clues (and eliminated more Lucian enemies) than any agent in history. When the leadership slipped Irina a name, that person disappeared within 24 hours. However, high-ranking sources inside the Lucian branch claim that the Kabras have ordered Irina to eliminate Amy and Dan . . . and yet they're still alive. Has Irina gone soft? Or is she simply waiting for the right moment to strike?

Last Will and Testament

I, Irina Nikolaievna Spaskaya, resident of Leningrad, USSR, being of sound mind and body, do declare this to be my last Will and Testament.

Bequests:

I leave everything to my beloved son, Nikolai Romanovich Spasky.

Bank accounts:

Russian Private Trust Bank, account no. 3754299399

Security Deposit Box: 12453 (Do not sell the jewels contained within until 2030. It should be safe by then.)

Swiss National Bank, account no. 98-3857-38668

Bank of the Cayman Islands, account no. 6543.4636.23455

Security Deposit Box: 7585 (Destroy this box without opening.)

My collection of valuable poisons and weapons. Sell to Boris Borisovich Bratsky. He's been wanting to get his hands on my tommy gun for years.

My apartment at No. 55 Fontanka Embankment. Push against a small button concealed in the fireplace and there is a secret stairway to a second apartment at No. 53 Fontanka Embankment. (Nikolai is NOT to enter the No. 53 apartment without adult supervision. And a bullet-proof vest.)

Signature: _Irina Spaskaya, 1988_

Amendment:

Due to the unforeseen death of Nikolai Romanovich Spasky, I now leave my possessions to the St. Petersburg Children's Theater with thanks for the hours of pleasure they gave my son.

Signature: _Irina Spaskaya, 1991_

AGENT FILE: KABRA, I.

IMPORTANT STATS

AGENT NAME: IAN KABRA

FAMILY BRANCH: LUCIAN

STATUS: HIGH; SON OF CURRENT LUCIAN LEADERS

HOMETOWN: LONDON, ENGLAND

AGE: 14

INTERESTS: POLO, SAILING, SKIING, GOURMET COFFEE

SKILLS: BRIBERY, BETRAYAL, POISON-MIXING

CLUE-HUNTING STRENGTHS: UNLIMITED FUNDS, PRIVATE JET, ACCESS TO TOP SECRET LUCIAN INTELLIGENCE.

WEAKNESS: VANITY. WHEN YOU'RE RACING TO SOME OF THE MOST TREACHEROUS LOCATIONS ON EARTH, SLIPPERY DESIGNER SHOES MAY NOT BE THE BEST IDEA.

Notes

A true Lucian, Ian has been raised to believe that nothing is more important than the Clues, which makes him a dangerous competitor. However, even he might be shocked to discover just how far his parents are willing to go. According to recent rumors, he's becoming a little uncomfortable with his mother's brutal tactics. Who knows what will happen if he ever discovers exactly what happened the night Hope and Arthur died. . . .

5 things IAN KABRA can't do without.

1. Custom-made shoes.

2. A full fuel tank in my private jet at all times. I have to be ready to travel on very short notice.

3. My polo ponies Bartholomew, Chauncey, and Clarence. Well, until they become too old to win. Then it's off to the glue factory.

4. Cell phone with global Internet access. I need to be able to e-mail from the top of Mount Everest if necessary.

5. A tranquilizer gun.

april: 2009

IMPORTANT STATS

AGENT NAME: NATALIE KABRA

FAMILY BRANCH: LUCIAN

STATUS: HIGH; DAUGHTER OF CURRENT LUCIAN LEADERS

HOMETOWN: LONDON, ENGLAND

AGE: 11

INTERESTS: SHOPPING, YACHTING, MANICURES, TARGET PRACTICE

SKILLS: DECEPTION, DEADLY AIM WITH A TRANQUILIZER GUN

CLUE-HUNTING STRENGTHS: UNLIMITED FUNDS, WORLD LEADERS ON ALL CONTINENTS TERRIFIED OF HER MOTHER

WEAKNESS: *EXTREME VANITY.* IT'S HARD TO SCRAMBLE DOWN THE STEPS OF AN ANCIENT EGYPTIAN TOMB IN STILETTOS.

Notes

Agents report that Natalie idolizes her mother, Isabel, and wants to be exactly like her. The two share stylish clothes, perfect hair, and a talent for poisoning. But there may be differences to exploit. Isabel has several known kills to her name, including a double murder. Natalie is not shy about using her poison dart gun (even on her English teacher) but currently has no blood on her hands. Will young Natalie be as ruthless as her mother, or could she be a possible candidate for our plan? More observation is necessary.

Dear diary,
I am so over this Clue-hunting rubbish.
I haven't gone shopping in, like, weeks. I actually
wore the same outfit twice last month! Ewww. What
if someone had seen me?!! I know finding the 39
Clues is important and like ultimate power
sounds lovely and all but a girl can only make so
many sacrifices.
 The pressure's getting to Ian as well. I think
he has a crush on AMY CAHILL. Ugh. I'm almost
too foul to imagine.
 How could he fancy some girl who dresses like a
color-blind homeless person?! Of course now I'll be able
to make Ian do whatever I want! He's afraid that I'll hack
into his CliqueMe page again. I changed his interests to
"girls who stutter, girls in ratty t-shirts, girls whose names
begin with "A," and orphans but not the cute kind!" It was
hilarious!!
            IK ♥ AC

Assorted
Letterhead
(for forging
Lucian letters)

LUCIAN

- FOLD -

- FOLD -

LUCIAN

------------------------------- FOLD -------------------------------

------------------------------- FOLD -------------------------------

LUCIAN

- F O L D -

- F O L D -

LUCIAN

FOLD

FOLD

ho your sole/h

EKATERINA

Ekaterina Branch

Current Branch Leader: Bae Oh (appointed after the tragic death of his twin brother, Gordon Oh)

Known Strongholds: unnamed island in Bermuda; Cairo, Egypt

Founder: Katherine Cahill

Famous Ekats: Marie Curie, Nikola Tesla, Thomas Edison

Characteristics: The world's most brilliant scientists, inventors, engineers, and archaeologists, the Ekaterinas are known for the sharpness of their brains and their single-minded focus. They've given the world the lightbulb, the telephone, and life-saving medicines . . . but also are responsible for building the atomic bomb.

Intelligence Report: Their genius IQs and cutting-edge spy technology make the Ekats serious Clue hunt contenders. The Ekaterina branch has come close to assembling the 39 Clues on several occasions. In Indonesia in 1883, they were only a few Clues away when the eruption of the volcano on Krakatoa destroyed their lab. The Ekaterina thinkers and scientists would be unstoppable if they could only work together. There are even rumors that the current branch leader, Bae Oh, murdered his own brother. . . .

Ekat Stronghold Location:
Bermuda

Invisible
Electric Fence

Landing Strip

Underground Fortified
Storage Facility

Bombproof
Laboratory

Torpedo
Launch Sites

Radar-Jamming
Transmitter

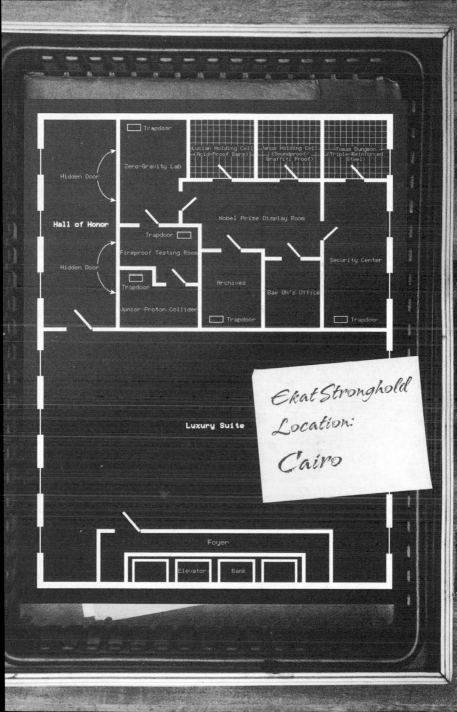

IMPORTANT STATS

AGENT NAME: KATHERINE CAHILL

FAMILY BRANCH: EKATERINA

STATUS: FOUNDER

HOMETOWN: IRELAND

SKILLS: REASONING, INVENTING, CALCULATING, ANALYZING, DOUBLE-CROSSING

SYMBOL: A DRAGON

PRIZED POSSESSION: A TELESCOPE

FAMOUS DESCENDANTS: GALILEO, MARIE CURIE, ALBERT EINSTEIN, HOWARD CARTER

Notes

From an early age, Katherine Cahill showed a remarkable aptitude for science. When she wasn't conducting experiments or observing the stars, she enjoyed exploring the Irish countryside with her brother Thomas. They spent countless hours imagining what it would be like to travel the world and promised that they would go on an adventure together someday. After their father died, Katherine and Thomas set off together, thrilled by the prospect of fulfilling their childhood dreams. However, when Thomas married and started a family, Katherine felt that her brother had deserted her. Angry and hurt, Katherine stole one of Thomas's Clues and ran away to Egypt, a land that had always fascinated her. Thomas never forgave his sister's treachery and, to this day, Tomas and Ekats are sworn enemies.

TOP SECRET

IMPORTANT STATS

AGENT NAME: ALISTAIR OH

FAMILY BRANCH: EKATERINA

STATUS: HIGH; SON OF FORMER LEADER, GORDON OH. NEPHEW OF CURRENT LEADER, BAE OH.

HOMETOWN: SEOUL, SOUTH KOREA

AGE: 64

INTERESTS: RESEARCHING NEW FLAVORS FOR MICROWAVABLE BURRITOS

SKILLS: THEFT, EXPLOSIVES, DOUBLE-CROSSING, TYING BOW TIES

CLUE-HUNTING STRENGTHS: WAS ONCE VERY CLOSE TO GRACE AND HOPE CAHILL AND KNOWS MANY OF THEIR SECRETS

WEAKNESS: HISTORY OF DECEPTION MAKES IT DIFFICULT TO FORM ALLIANCES

Notes

Ever since his father, Gordon, was mysteriously murdered, Alistair has been the black sheep of the Ekaterina branch. His uncle, Ekat leader Bae Oh, loves to remind Alistair of his failures: his expulsion from Harvard, his bankrupted burrito business, etc. However, Alistair was always close to his cousin Grace and then her daughter, Hope. He was devastated when she and her husband were killed in a fire. He keeps trying to forget the tragic "accident," but certain memories won't be erased. Guilt is a powerful preservative.

HOPE, MY DEAR!

HOW DELIGHTFUL TO GET YOUR LETTER AND THE
PHOTOS OF YOUNG DANIEL. YOU WEREN'T MUCH OLDER WHEN WE
FIRST MET. AH, HOW LONG AGO IT SEEMS!

I MUST SAY I WAS SURPRISED TO HEAR THAT YOU ARE
GIVING UP YOUR "TRAVELS." I WISH I COULD SAY I BELIEVED YOU,
BUT I HEAR RUMORS THAT YOU AND ARTHUR WERE RECENTLY IN
CAIRO. NAUGHTY, NAUGHTY! MY DEAR GIRL, DID YOU REALLY
THINK YOU'D GET ONE PAST YOUR UNCLE ALISTAIR? AS AGREED,
EGYPT IS MY TERRITORY.

AH, WELL! NO HARD FEELINGS, OF COURSE! IN FACT, I'M
IN MEXICO NOW, RESEARCHING BURRITO FLAVORS. MY RETURN
FLIGHT TAKES ME THROUGH BOSTON, AND I'LL BE IN YOUR FAIR
CITY ON MAY 15. SHALL I TAKE YOU AND ARTHUR OUT TO
DINNER THAT NIGHT?

YOURS AFFECTIONATELY,
ALISTAIR

Statement of Witness

BOSTON POLICE DEPARTMENT

Statement taken

on __5.15.01__

at witnesses

~~Home~~/ __Boston__
__Police Station__

by

__Det. Brown__

No. __117__

Description

Ht _____

Wt _____

Hair _____

Other _____

FOR OFFICAL USE ONLY

Enq. Form _____

No. _____

Working Statement

No. _____

Guide Card

No. _____

Form MC235

FULL NAME: _Alistair Oh_

AGE: _57_

Occupation: _Inventor_

This ~~event~~ tragedy was a terrible ~~mistake~~
accident. I'm not sure what happened.
I only arrived on the scene at ~~10~~ 11:30pm
for a late visit. I ~~always~~ sometimes ~~visit~~
5   visited Hope and Arthur when in Boston.
I can't imagine what ~~went wrong~~ happened.
This was not ~~part of the plan~~ supposed to
happen. I don't ~~think~~ know what else to tell
you. This is just awful. I'm sorry.
10   I don't

15

EKATERINA

IMPORTANT STATS

AGENT NAME: BAE OH

FAMILY BRANCH: EKATERINA

STATUS: HIGH; BRANCH LEADER

HOMETOWN: SEOUL, SOUTH KOREA

AGE: 87

INTERESTS: OPERA, SURVEILLANCE TECHNIQUES, ROBOTICS, UNLIMITED POWER

SKILLS: CONSPIRACIES, COVER-UPS, BETRAYAL

CLUE-HUNTING STRENGTHS: ACCESS TO THE MOST ADVANCED TECHNOLOGY ON EARTH

WEAKNESS: SPENDS MORE TIME TRACKING HIS NEPHEW ALISTAIR'S FAILURES THAN HE DOES WORKING TOWARD EKAT SUCCESSES

AGENT FILE: OH, B.

Notes

As a young man, Bae Oh was constantly overshadowed by his twin brother, Gordon. While Bae squandered his inheritance, Gordon devoted himself to the family business and the Clue hunt. Yet, despite his laziness, Bae craved power. According to reports, he was furious when Gordon was chosen to be the head of the Ekaterina branch. However, Gordon's period of leadership came to a tragic end when he was accidentally shot during a robbery. Bae took over for his brother and has held the post ever since. Is it because he is such a talented leader? Or does it have more to do with the fact that all of Bae's rivals die in similar mysterious accidents?

OH INDUSTRIES

April 22, 1948

Dear ██████████████

Brother will be arriving on 15:07 Delta flight, Idlewild Airport in New York, May 11. Booked into Room 1501 at Waldorf Astoria on Park Avenue. Scheduled to meet car in front of hotel on May 12 at 7:15 P.M., after dinner, for trip to Broadway play at Imperial Theater. Driver is ██████████████. Will take route across 45th Street.

Upon completion of mission, payment will be forwarded by the expected means. Please confirm $5K US as proper amount. Destroy letter immediately.

Sincerely,

Bae Oh
Senior Vice President

Victim Gordon Oh

Assorted
Letterhead

(to forge
Ekat letters)

- FOLD -

- FOLD -

---------------------------------- F O L D ----------------------------------

---------------------------------- F O L D ----------------------------------

------------------- F O L D -------------------

------------------- F O L D -------------------

FOLD

FOLD

TOMAS

Tomas Branch

Current Branch Leader: Ivan Kleister

Known Strongholds: Mt. Fuji, Japan and Mt. Eden, New Zealand

Founder: Thomas Cahill

Famous Tomas: George Washington, Annie Oakley, Meriwether Lewis & William Clark

Characteristics: The Tomas are renowned for their athleticism. They're the strongest, fastest, and most coordinated people on earth. Almost any legendary athlete you can name was a Tomas, from baseball players to jujitsu masters. They're also known for their bravery and sense of adventure; the branch produced the most famous explorers in history. They were always the first to cross oceans, chart continents, and scale treacherous mountains. And as one might expect, they're fiercely competitive. For the Tomas, it's not whether you win or lose, but how long it takes your opponents to stop crying.

Intelligence Report: Tomas athleticism and taste for adventure poses a challenge for agents from other branches. Many of the Tomas Clues are hidden in the most extreme locations on earth, spots that require incredible strength and bravery to access. There are some shortcuts, though. The Tomas's sworn rivals, the Ekaterinas, develop technology for the sole purpose of stealing their enemies' Clues. After centuries of being dismissed for being all brawn and no brains, the Tomas are ready to show the Cahills what they can do. Their pride and competitiveness make them dangerous adversaries, especially when it's no longer a game.

Tomas Stronghold Location:
Mt. Fuji

IMPORTANT STATS

AGENT NAME: THOMAS CAHILL

FAMILY BRANCH: TOMAS

STATUS: FOUNDER

HOMETOWN: IRELAND

SKILLS: STRENGTH, ATHLETICISM, BRAVERY, NAVIGATION

SYMBOL: A POLAR BEAR

PRIZED POSSESSION: A COMPASS

FAMOUS DESCENDANTS: GEORGE WASHINGTON, ANNIE OAKLEY, JESSE OWENS

AGENT FILE: CAHILL, T.

Notes

Growing up, Thomas never fully understood his siblings' obsession with their father's research. He was intrigued by the idea of absolute power but wasn't willing to fight his family to achieve it. Unlike Luke, he never spied on Gideon. Nor did he approve of Katherine's schemes. However, the fire changed Thomas. He was appalled to think that Luke's ambition might have led to their father's death, and he took solace in the belief that Katherine would have never gone so far. He was happy to leave Ireland with Katherine and believed she was the only sibling he could fully trust. For Thomas, loyalty became the most important quality of all. When Katherine ran away, taking one of his Clues with her, Thomas was destroyed and pledged revenge. Ever since, the Tomas have been devoted Clue hunters. They'll never let anyone take advantage of them again.

TOP SECRET

IMPORTANT STATS

AGENT NAME: HAMILTON HOLT

FAMILY BRANCH: TOMAS

STATUS: LOW; SON OF TOMAS OUTCAST, EISENHOWER HOLT

HOMETOWN: MILWAUKEE, USA

AGE: 15

INTERESTS: FOOTBALL, COMPUTER PROGRAMMING, BASEBALL, SOCCER, VIDEO GAMES

SKILLS: COMPUTER HACKING, INTIMIDATION, URBAN CLIMBING

CLUE-HUNTING STRENGTHS: THE HOLTS ARE THE BLACK SHEEP OF THE TOMAS BRANCH, WHICH MEANS OTHER TEAMS WON'T SEE THEM AS A THREAT

WEAKNESS: AFRAID TO STAND UP TO HIS FATHER, EVEN WHEN HAMILTON HAS A BETTER IDEA

Notes

The Tomas leadership has been monitoring Hamilton for years. His athleticism combined with his computer skills makes him an ideal agent. However, according to reports, Hamilton cares more about impressing his father than he does about finding the 39 Clues. Hamilton's need for approval could become a useful tool for his enemies. He will be easy to manipulate, unless the hunt for the 39 Clues makes Hamilton question Eisenhower's methods. The one sound that could ring louder than his father's referee whistle is the voice of his own conscience.

THOMPSON FALLS
MIDDLE SCHOOL

REPORT CARD

Name: Hamilton Holt
Homeroom: Mrs. McNulty

Grade: 9

Class: Biology
Teacher: Mr. Gunther
Grade: C -
Comments: Hamilton needs to control his temper. I don't care
if the model skeleton was giving him a "funny look." It
is never acceptable to hurl school property out the window.

Class: English
Teacher: Mr. Chang
Grade: D
Comments: After spending 10 months in a classroom with Hamilton,
I'm still not sure whether he knows how to read.

Class: Advanced Computer Lab
Teacher: Mrs. Goldstein
Grade: B
Comments: Hamilton has done great work this semester, but I had to
take points off for behavior. The computer lab is no place to play
basketball, especially when it involves tossing Jimmy Littleman into
the trash can.

Class: Geometry
Teacher: Ms. Gonzalez
Grade: D
Comments: I wish Hamilton had spent more time taking notes
and less time hanging Jimmy Littleman from the ceiling.

Class: Gym
Teacher: Coach Warner
Grade: A +
Comments: Hamilton is the most gifted athlete I've ever coached.
He excels at every sport. He even mastered synchronized swimming but
told me that he would "pulverize me" if I told anyone!

TOP SECRET

IMPORTANT STATS

AGENT NAME: REAGAN HOLT

FAMILY BRANCH: TOMAS

STATUS: LOW; DAUGHTER OF TOMAS OUTCAST, EISENHOWER HOLT

HOMETOWN: MILWAUKEE, USA

AGE: 11

INTERESTS: SOCCER, PURPLE TRACK SUITS, BASKETBALL, BALLET?

SKILLS: EXPLOSIVES, KIDNAPPING, HIDING SECRET HOBBIES

CLUE-HUNTING STRENGTHS: CAN PRETEND TO BE A CUTE ELEVEN-YEAR-OLD WHEN SHE NEEDS TO BE. DOESN'T HESITATE TO PLACE FULL-GROWN ADULTS IN A HEADLOCK, WHEN NECESSARY

WEAKNESS: HAS SPENT MORE TIME IN DETENTION THAN IN THE CLASSROOM

Notes

Reagan and her twin sister, Madison, are universally feared by their classmates, teammates, and the neighborhood dogs. (Authorities are still investigating the incident of the substitute teacher who was strung up a flagpole.) However, spies report that Reagan doesn't take quite as much pleasure from terrorizing people as Madison does. She loves ballet but is afraid of letting her siblings discover her secret hobby. (The Holts don't approve of sports without full body contact.) It will be interesting to observe Reagan on the hunt. Will she convince her family to be a little less brutal? Or will her fear of being teased cause her to be the most vicious Holt of all?

Dear Diary,
    Tomorrow is my birthday
    and I really hope I get
    ballet slippers. But then
    Madison will know that
    I've actually been taking
    ballet, not jujitsu.
She and Ham won't stop laughing
for a gazillion years.
    They already think I'm going soft
because I don't want to play
full contact checkers with
the old people at the senior
center anymore.

Wish me luck!

*Pages stolen from
Reagan's diary*

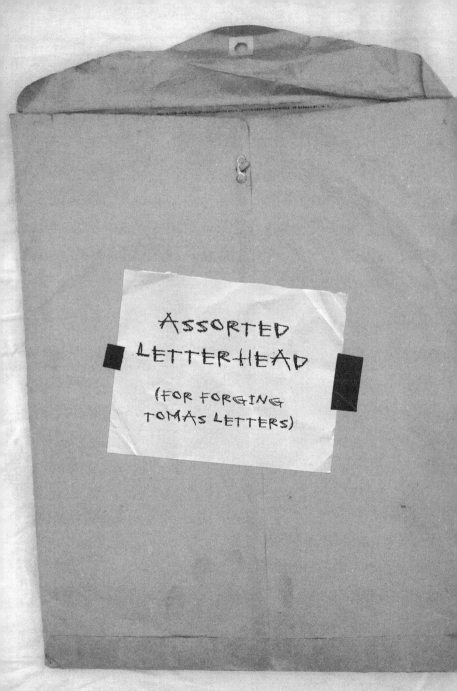

- F O L D - - - - - - - - - - - - - - - -

- F O L D - - - - - - - - - - - - - - - -

------------------------------- F O L D -----------------------------------

------------------------------- F O L D -----------------------------------

- FOLD -

- FOLD -

- F O L D -

- F O L D -

- F O L D -

- F O L D -

Janus Branch

Current Branch Leader: Cora Wizard

Known Strongholds: Hollywood, USA; Venice, Italy

Founder: Jane Cahill

Famous Janus: Thomas Jefferson, Wolfgang Amadeus Mozart, Jane Austen, Pablo Picasso

Characteristics: The Janus are exceptionally creative. They excel at drawing, writing, music, acting, dancing—any art form you can name and some you can't even imagine. (Who knew you could teach an octopus to finger paint?) The other branches sometimes underestimate the Janus. They believe their artistic cousins are too busy focusing on art to have any chance of finding the 39 Clues. But the Janus's rivals forget that there are many forms of creativity. While some Janus design buildings, others figure out how to break into them. Some invent stories, others invent deadly booby traps.

Intelligence Report: The most creative people are often the most dangerous, and the Janus are no exception. When the Janus decide to eliminate an enemy, they devise dozens of plans, each more treacherous than the last. And while they have slightly less experience than their Lucian cousins in trying to take over the world, the Janus honestly think that they deserve to rule. Their current leader, Cora Wizard, thinks the Janus time has come and will stop at nothing to find the 39 Clues—the key to ultimate power.

Architectural Drawing of
the Janus Hollywood Stronghold

IMPORTANT STATS

AGENT NAME: JANE CAHILL

FAMILY BRANCH: JANUS

STATUS: FOUNDER

HOMETOWN: IRELAND

SKILLS: PAINTING, WRITING, SINGING, COMPOSING, DRAWING

SYMBOL: A WOLF

PRIZED POSSESSION: A HARP

FAMOUS DESCENDANTS: WOLFGANG AMADEUS MOZART, JANE AUSTEN, MARY SHELLEY, JOSEPHINE BAKER

AGENT FILE: CAHILL, J.

Notes

The youngest of Gideon Cahill's children, Jane always looked up to her older siblings. She admired Thomas's adventurous spirit and Katherine's inquisitive mind. In particular, she worshipped her oldest brother, Luke. He always went out of his way to care for Jane and delighted in hearing her music or reading her poetry. When Jane saw him in Gideon's burning lab, she was heartbroken. In the years that followed, she devoted herself to her work in attempt to forget the pain of losing her family. Her descendants continued her commitment to art, believing that nothing was more important than beauty and expression. Nothing, that is, except finding the 39 Clues. The Janus can be as ruthless and conniving as any of the Cahills and are willing to do whatever it takes to come out on top.

TOP SECRET

IMPORTANT STATS

AGENT NAME: JONAH WIZARD

FAMILY BRANCH: JANUS

STATUS: HIGH; SON OF CURRENT LEADER, CORA WIZARD

HOMETOWN: LOS ANGELES, USA

AGE: 15

INTERESTS: SOLD-OUT CONCERTS, RED CARPETS, REARRANGING HIS GRAMMY AWARDS

SKILLS: SONGWRITING, SINGING, RAPPING, CREATING DIVERSIONS, BREAKING INTO HIGH-SECURITY VAULTS

CLUE-HUNTING STRENGTHS: MILLIONS OF FANS WORLDWIDE WILLING TO DO ANYTHING FOR HIS AUTOGRAPH

WEAKNESS: CAN'T GO ANYWHERE WITHOUT THE PAPARAZZI FOLLOWING HIM

Notes

At 15, Jonah is one of the most famous entertainers in the world. His face is plastered on billboards, magazine covers, and countless souvenir items, from T-shirts to special edition Jonah Wizard back scratchers. However, sources report that his mother, Cora, isn't overly impressed with his success. She wants Jonah to find the 39 Clues in addition to going on world tours and filming his hit television show. Will Jonah crack under the pressure? Or will his intense desire to earn Cora's approval make him a danger to other Cahills on the hunt?

AGENT FILE: WIZARD, J.

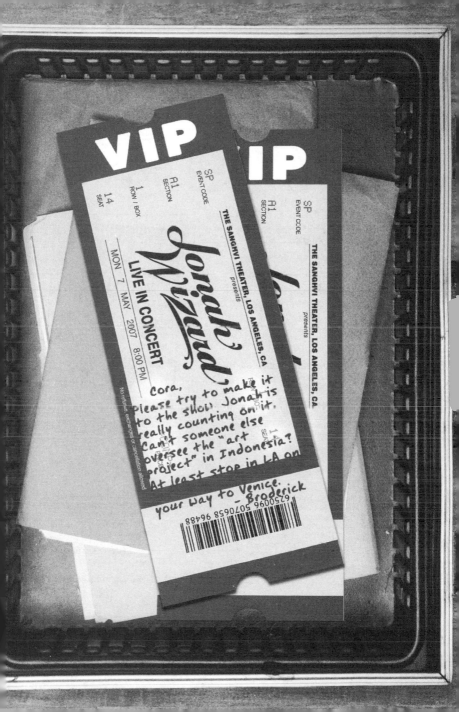

TOP SECRET

IMPORTANT STATS

AGENT NAME: CORA WIZARD

FAMILY BRANCH: JANUS

STATUS: HIGH; BRANCH LEADER

HOMETOWN: HOLLYWOOD, USA

INTERESTS: ABSTRACT ART,
EXPERIMENTAL THEATER, UNIQUE
JEWELRY

SKILLS: PAINTING, SCULPTURE,
MANIPULATION, DRAWING, SPYING,
BLACKMAIL

CLUE-HUNTING STRENGTHS:
THOUSANDS OF JANUS AGENTS WHO
FIND HER TERRIFYING

WEAKNESS: HAS DIFFICULTY
RECOGNIZING TALENT IN OTHERS,
ESPECIALLY WHEN THEY'RE RELATED
TO HER

Notes

Under Cora Wizard's leadership, the Janus branch has become a major
force on the Clue hunt. She upgraded the surveillance technology
(stolen from the Ekats) in the Hollywood and Venice strongholds and
has agents monitoring Clue locations around the world. She knows that
the famous Janus creativity alone won't be enough to ensure victory,
so she trains her agents to be as sneaky as the Lucians. However, some
Cahills feel that Cora went too far that night in Boston. The fire that
killed Hope Cahill and Arthur Trent might have been an accident. But
then why couldn't Cora look Grace in the eye at Hope and Arthur's
funeral?

Talent Identification

Use this form to help identify artistic skills
in Janus children.

Name: Jonah Wizard
Age: 3

Talent: Painting
Genius Gifted Skilled Mediocre (Little Talent)
Comments: *painted the dog instead of the canvas*

Talent: Sculpture
Genius Gifted Skilled Mediocre (Little Talent)
Comments: *ate the clay*

Talent: Collage
Genius Gifted Skilled Mediocre (Little Talent)
Comments: *glued fingers together*

Overall comments: *Will try music next. I know my
son's going to be a star.*

— Cora

Assorted
Letterhead

(to forge Janus letters)

- FOLD -

- FOLD -

- FOLD -

- FOLD -

FOLD

FOLD

- F O L D -

- F O L D -

CLASSIFIED

CODES:

Sneaky Ways to Pass
Top Secret Information

TOP
SECRET

I think this is the key.
abcdefghijklmnopqrstuvwxyz
- - - - - W - - Z - - - - - - - - - - - - KL - - - - - -

code 1:
CSLZWJAFW SFV LZGESK

_____

(Solution)

code 2:
OWJW OJGFY STGML DMCW

_____

(Solution)

Create your own code:

_____

_____

_____

_____

_____

code 1:

26-12-15-15-12-4-16 16-6-12-17-23-2-21-8

_____
(Solution)

code 2:

12-22 17-18-23 13-24-22-23 4 15-4-26-2-8-21

_____
(Solution)

Create your own code:

_____

_____

_____

_____

_____

fig. 1

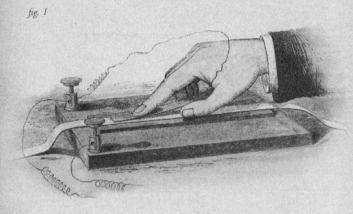

fig. 2

THE INTERNATIONAL MORSE TELEGRAPH ALPHABET.

A	B	C	D	E	F	G
·—	—···	—·—·	—··	·	··—·	——·
H	I	J	K	L	M	N
····	··	·———	—·—	·—··	——	—·
O	P	Q	R	S	T	U
———	·——·	——·—	·—·	···	—	··—
V	W	X	Y	Z		
···—	·——	—··—	—·——	——··		

Ä	Ö	Ü	Ch
·—·—	———·	··——	————

Numerals.

0	1	2	3	4
—————	·————	··———	···——	····—
5	6	7	8	9
·····	—····	——···	———··	————·

Punctuation.

Period (.)	Comma (,)	Colon (:)	Question Mark (?)
·—·—·—	——··——	———···	··——··
Exclamation Point (!)	Quotation (")	Apostrophe (')	Equals (=)
··——·—	·—··—·	·————·	—···—

CODE 1:

-..-/---/.-.•/.- •--/.-/••• -/••••/•/.--./

_____

(Solution)

CODE 2:

•--/••••/•/-• -/••••/• ••-•/••/.--•/• -•••/••-/.--/-•/•/--•••

_____

(Solution)

Create your own code:

_____

_____

_____

_____

_____

INTERNATIONAL SIGNAL FL...

code 1:

_____
(Solution)

code 2:

_____
(Solution)

Create your own code:

_____

_____

_____

_____

THE EMPIRE STATE HERALD

Dear Henry,

We have a task tat only you ar
fit for. Dr. David Livingstone
as been missing for so long tht
no one care ny longer. We an't
sell any more newspapers until
there are new deveopments.
We're sending you to Africa to
find him. If you're clever, you
may find something even more
valabl than a missing missionary.

Yours Sincerely,

James Gordon Bennett
James Gordon Bennett

code 1:

I suspec tat somene has been looking
through y mil. All future mesages hould b
sen in code. I will leave out key leters.
Write out the missing ettrs and you will
know the meaning behind my wors.

——————————————————————————

(Solution)

code 2:

Sr Hery Morton Stanley. named ohn
Rowlands by his prents, had a taste for
exloration nd jouralism.

——————————————————————————

(Solution)

Create your own code:

——————————————————————————

——————————————————————————

——————————————————————————

ИМПЕРАТОРСКІЙ Телеграфъ Екатеринбург, Россія

ТЕЛЕГРАММА № 289

13 Словъ

А (A)	З (Z)	М (M)	Т (T)
Б (B)	И (I)	Н (N)	У (U)
В (V)	Й (Y)	О (O)	Ф (F)
Г (G)		П (P)	Х (H)
Д (D)	К (K)	Р (R)	Э (E)
Е (E)	Л (L)	С (S)	

code 1:

АНАСТАСИА НО ЛОНГЕР СУРВИВЕС

_____

(Solution)

code 2:

БУТ ХЕР КИД ДОЕС

_____

(Solution)

Create your own code:

_____

_____

_____

_____

CODE 1:

_____

(SOLUTION)

CODE 2:

_____

(SOLUTION)

CREATE YOUR OWN CODE:

_____

_____

_____

_____

_____

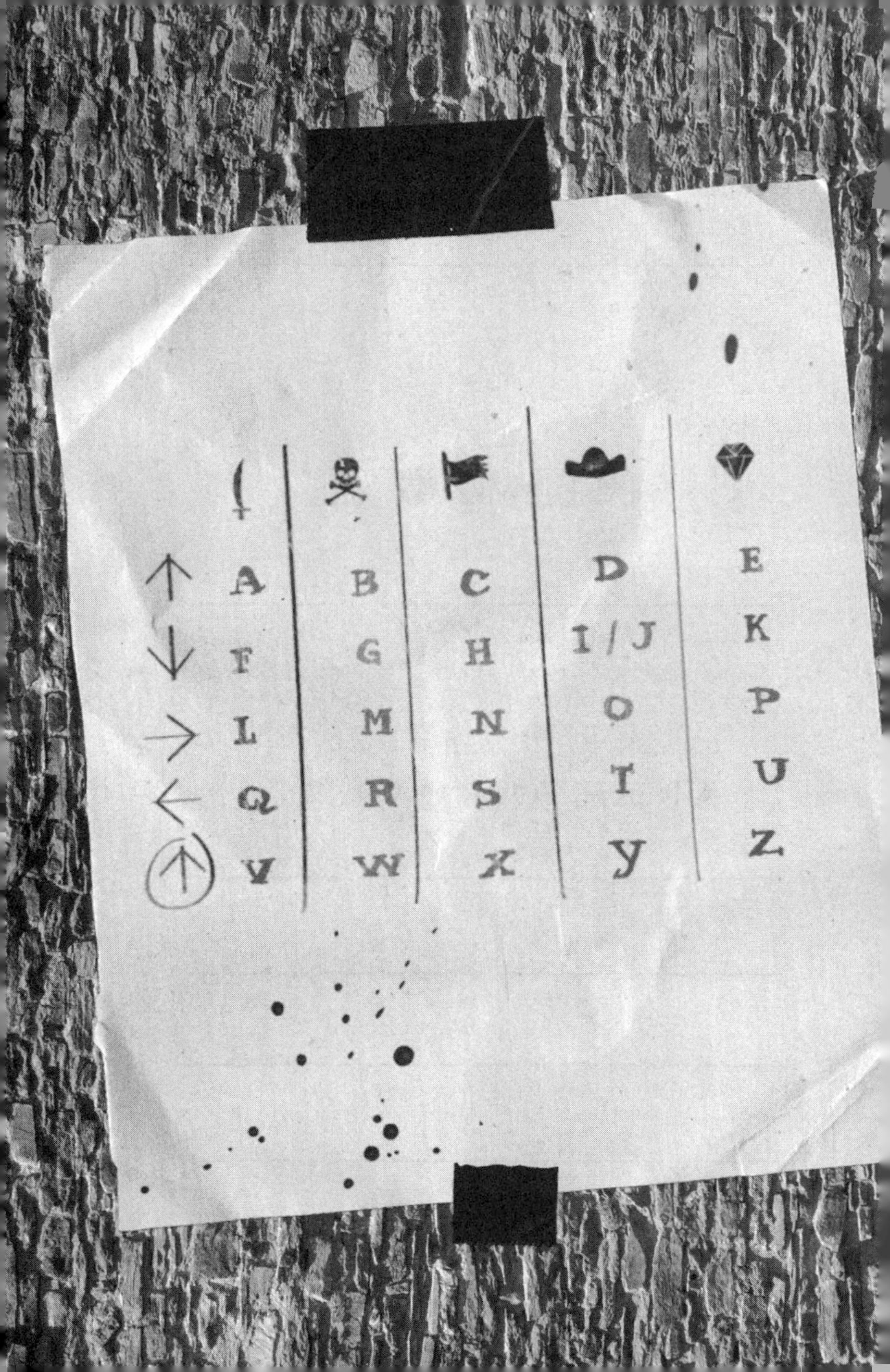
A B C D E
F G H I/J K
L M N O P
Q R S T U
V W X Y Z

code 1:

_____
(Solution)

code 2:

_____
(Solution)

Create your own code:

_____

_____

_____

_____

CONFIDENTIAL

TO: ALL LUCIANS

RE: NEW CODES

At least one of the other branches has cracked our codes. The spies will be caught and eliminated but we still need to be careful.

Be extra vigilant! Moving forward, Lucians should write everything (including love letters, notes to teachers, and shopping lists) in one of the new codes:

• **Every Other Letter Code:** Read every other letter, starting with the first, then go back and put together the letters you missed:

Example:

Hooiwn agrteo ydoau? = How are you?

Try this one on your own for practice:
nsetv aenre tkraut srtqan npeak vast

• **Pigpen Code:** Put letters in a tic-tac-toe board and around an X as follows:

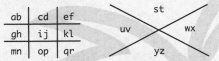

Each letter is represented by the part of the "pigpen" that surrounds it. A dot refers to the second letter in the space.

Example:

A looks like this: ⌐|

B looks like this: ⌐•|

Z looks like this: /•\

See if you can decode this phrase:

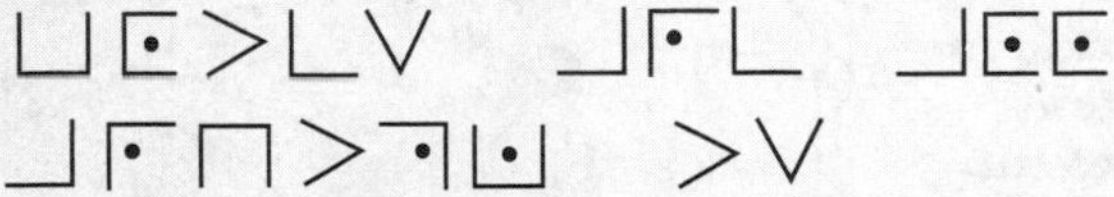

⊔●>�ⱽ ⌐⌐●⌐ ⌐●●
⌐●⊓>⌐⊔● >ⱽ

● **Route Cipher:** Hide your message in a box of random letters and symbols. Then create a route to find it.

Practice on the cipher below. The route is:

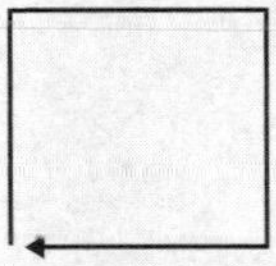

E I N F O R C E

R D E ? ? ? ? M

D S I B K P Q E

N Y & U N I I N

E H E L I O C T

S ! ! ! W O N S

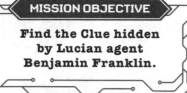

BOOK ONE

THE MAZE OF BONES

MISSION OBJECTIVE

Find the Clue hidden by Lucian agent Benjamin Franklin.

Agents Involved:

Amy and Dan Cahill (unknown)
Ian and Natalie Kabra (Lucian)
Jonah Wizard (Janus)
Alistair Oh (Ekat)
Irina Spasky (Lucian)
The Starlings (Ekat)
The Holts (Tomas)

Locations:

- **Philadelphia,** USA
- **Paris,** France

Tools Required:

- Black light
- High-powered battery
- Poison fingernails
- Surveillance bugs

Intelligence report:

The first stage of the plan was a success. Amy and Dan attended their grandmother's will reading and learned that they belong to the most powerful family in history—the Cahills. Per the terms of Grace's will, they were presented with a choice between a million dollars and the first Clue. As we hoped, they chose the Clue. The children exceeded expectations by decoding the hint and then headed to Philadelphia to research Benjamin Franklin. They followed a lead to Paris and followed the trail to a secret location under the city, where they were cornered by the other teams. Whether by skill or sheer luck, Amy and Dan made it out alive and somehow managed to hold on to the Clue. However, their early success might lead to their downfall. Their rivals now view Amy and Dan as a threat, and there's no knowing how far the other Cahills will go to eliminate the competition.

INFORMATION DISCOVERED

Clue: _____

My Notes on Rival Agents: _____
_____
_____
_____

Hints Gathered on Future Clue Locations: _____
_____
_____
_____

New Cahill Founder Identified: _____
_____
_____
_____

New Information Uncovered: _____
_____
_____
_____

MISSION OBJECTIVE

Discover Mozart's most dangerous secret.

Agents Involved:

Amy and Dan Cahill (unknown)
Ian and Natalie Kabra (Lucian)
Jonah Wizard (Janus)
Alistair Oh (Ekat)
Irina Spasky (Lucian)
The Holts (Tomas)

Locations:

- **Vienna,** Austria
- **Salzburg,** Austria
- **Venice,** Italy

Challenges:

- Break into a four-star hotel
- Steal a two-hundred-year-old journal
- Flee a horde of angry monks
- Escape a cave-in
- Survive a high-speed boat chase
- Explode a piano

Intelligence report:

After decoding a hint hidden in sheet music, Amy and Dan traveled to Vienna and Salzburg to trace the footsteps of Janus composer Wolfgang Amadeus Mozart. After their close call in Paris, the children were slightly more cautious, but they still stumbled into a trap set by one of their competitors. It's a miracle they escaped from that cave-in alive. The children fell off our radar afterwards, but sources report that they were seen in Venice, near the home of a crucial Janus founder. We haven't yet received confirmation, but there are rumors that the Kabras launched a sneak attack on Amy and Dan. No word yet on which team found the Clue.

INFORMATION DISCOVERED

Clue: _____

My Notes on Rival Agents: _____
_____
_____
_____

Hints Gathered on Future Clue Locations: _____
_____
_____
_____

New Cahill Founder Identified: _____
_____
_____
_____

New Information Uncovered: _____
_____
_____
_____

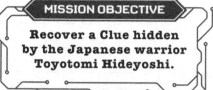

BOOK THREE

THE SWORD THIEF

MISSION OBJECTIVE

Recover a Clue hidden by the Japanese warrior Toyotomi Hideyoshi.

Agents Involved:

Amy and Dan Cahill (unknown)
Ian and Natalie Kabra (Lucian)
Alistair Oh (Ekat)
Irina Spasky (Lucian)
The Holts (Tomas)

Locations:

- **Tokyo,** Japan
- **Seoul,** South Korea

Secrets revealed:

- Faked death
- Identity theft
- Look-alike decoys
- Computer hacking
- Backstabbing and heartbreaking

Intelligence report:

Amy and Dan formed an alliance with Alistair Oh and accompanied him on a private jet. Flight records reveal that they flew to Tokyo. According to a stolen Lucian agent report, Amy and Dan agreed to a temporary alliance with Ian and Natalie Kabra. (This information needs to be confirmed, as it's highly improbable. It might be a Lucian trick.) The group followed a lead to South Korea, on the trail of a legendary hiding spot. That's where our intelligence gets a little fuzzy. There are rumors that the Kabras betrayed Amy and Dan and stole the Clue, but there is no evidence to support that claim. Further investigation is necessary.

INFORMATION DISCOVERED

Clue: _____

My Notes on Rival Agents: _____

_____

_____

_____

Hints Gathered on Future Clue Locations: _____

_____

_____

_____

New Cahill Founder Identified: _____

_____

_____

_____

New Information Uncovered: _____

_____

_____

_____

BOOK FOUR

BEYOND THE GRAVE

MISSION OBJECTIVE

Find a Clue hidden by Ekaterina founder Katherine Cahill.

Agents Involved:

Amy and Dan Cahill (unknown)
Alistair Oh (Ekat)
Irina Spasky (Lucian)
Jonah Wizard (Janus)

Locations:

- **Cairo**, Egypt
- **Luxor**, Egypt
- **Final location unknown**

Past attempts:

- **Napoleon Bonaparte** (late 18th century)
- **Winston Churchill** (mid 20th century)

Challenges:

- Break into an Egyptian tomb
- Recover a priceless artifact
- Survive an ancient curse
- Outrun a crocodile
- Explore underwater ruins
- Avoid the Madrigals . . .

Intelligence report:

Amy and Dan traveled to Egypt on the trail of a long-lost Clue that, according to Cahill legend, was hidden by Katherine Cahill sometime in the 16th century. (For hundreds of years, agents from all branches have scoured the country. Napoleon Bonaparte even led his army into Egypt in pursuit.) According to stolen Ekat intelligence, Amy and Dan snuck into the Ekaterina stronghold in Cairo and barely made it out alive. They then followed a lead to Luxor, where they managed to break into an ancient tomb—no small feat, even for a Cahill. After escaping a trap set by one of their rivals, the children fell off our radar. The most recent reports suggest that none of the teams found the Clue in Egypt. It's been hidden for too many centuries, and crucial hints have disappeared. However, it's difficult to believe that Grace Cahill did not account for this. She might have laid plans yet to be revealed.

INFORMATION DISCOVERED

Clue: _____

My Notes on Rival Agents: _____
_____
_____
_____

Hints Gathered on Future Clue Locations: _____
_____
_____
_____

New Cahill Founder Identified: _____
_____
_____
_____

New Information Uncovered: _____
_____
_____
_____

BOOK FIVE

THE BLACK CIRCLE

MISSION OBJECTIVE

Find the Amber Room and discover the truth about a lost princess.

Agents Involved:

Amy and Dan Cahill (unknown)
Ian and Natalie Kabra (Lucian)
Irina Spasky (Lucian)
The Holts (Tomas)

Locations:

- **Volgograd,** Russia
- **St. Petersburg,** Russia
- **Moscow,** Russia
- **Yekaterinburg,** Russia
- **Magadan,** Russia
- **Omsk,** Russia

Secrets revealed:

- Motorcycle
- Fake passports / Disguises
- Tiny Russian car
- KAMAZ truck
- Visa Gold Card
- World's fastest helicopter

Intelligence report:

In Cairo, Amy and Dan received a mysterious package from an anonymous person known only as NRR. It included two tickets to Russia in addition to a photo of their parents, Hope Cahill and Arthur Trent, in Moscow. Although they knew it could be a trap, the children couldn't turn down the chance to learn about their parents' tie to the 39 Clues. In Russia, Amy and Dan realized the Clue was related to the Amber Room, which disappeared during World War II. They followed a number of leads around the country, unaware that NRR was monitoring them the whole time. When they finally reached Moscow, the danger was so immense we decided to break protocol and warn the children. But it was too late. Their urge to learn about their parents overwhelmed their reason. NRR's plan succeeded. It is unclear whether Amy and Dan found the Clue before they escaped. Or if they made it out at all.

INFORMATION DISCOVERED

Clue: _____

My Notes on Rival Agents: _____
_____
_____
_____

Hints Gathered on Future Clue Locations: _____
_____
_____
_____

New Cahill Founder Identified: _____
_____
_____
_____

New Information Uncovered: _____
_____
_____
_____

BOOK SIX

IN TOO DEEP

Agents Involved:

Amy and Dan Cahill (unknown)
Alistair Oh (Ekat)
Irina Spasky (Lucian)
Ian and Natalie Kabra (Lucian)
The Holts (Tomas)

Locations:

- **Sydney,** Australia
- **Coober Pedy,** Australia
- **Darwin,** Australia
- **Jakarta,** Indonesia
- **Final location unknown**

Secrets revealed:

- Amelia Earhart's real plan
- The truth about the fire that killed Hope Cahill and Arthur Trent
- The secret that changed Irina forever
- The reason for Hope and Arthur's mysterious trips
- How to survive an encounter with the deadliest creatures on earth

Intelligence report:

After discovering Hope and Arthur's fake Australian passports in a Lucian vault, Amy and Dan traveled Down Under to retrace their parents' steps. (Fortunately, they haven't discovered Hope and Arthur's real secret. We must keep it from them as long as possible, or our plan will fail.) The Kabras had been tracking Amy and Dan and arrived shortly after. They followed the children as they researched Amelia Earhart and the secret behind her plane's mysterious disappearance. However, this time, Isabel Kabra was with them. It was worrying to discover that she's now handling the Clue hunt personally. The competition was dangerous before. Now it's only a matter of time before the hunt yields its first casualty. In fact, there are rumors of a terrible accident in Indonesia, but there's no trustworthy information at this time. We will continue to monitor the situation.

INFORMATION DISCOVERED

Clue: _____

My Notes on Rival Agents: _____
_____
_____
_____
_____

Hints Gathered on Future Clue Locations: _____
_____
_____
_____
_____

New Cahill Founder Identified: _____
_____
_____
_____
_____

New Information Uncovered: _____
_____
_____
_____
_____

BOOK SEVEN

THE VIPER'S NEST

MISSION OBJECTIVE

Discover a Clue related to the legendary Tomas warrior Shaka Zulu.

Agents Involved:

Amy and Dan Cahill (unknown)
Alistair Oh (Ekat)
Ian and Natalie Kabra (Lucian)
The Holts (Tomas)

Locations:

- **Pretoria,** South Africa
- **Johannesburg,** South Africa
- **Witbank,** South Africa
- **Durban,** South Africa
- **Final location unknown**

Secrets revealed:

- The location of Grace's hidden stronghold
- The reason why Hope and Arthur were suspected of murder
- Which Cahills were present the night Hope and Arthur died
- Amy and Dan's branch

Intelligence report:

After recovering from the tragic events in Indonesia, Amy and Dan flew to South Africa on the trail of the Tomas Clue related to Shaka Zulu. The children were performing well until they came across some shocking information about their parents. (Fortunately, Amy and Dan brushed it off as a misunderstanding. They are still not ready for the truth.) They followed a lead to Durban, where, according to stolen security data, they broke into the Tomas stronghold. It is hard to believe that Grace would've purposely led her grandchildren into such a dangerous situation, but Amy and Dan exceeded expectations—they somehow made it out alive. However, the children were apprehended by the Kabras before they could leave South Africa. We believe they escaped, but we haven't yet identified their exact location. Flight logs suggest that they went to Grace's secret stronghold, but there is no need to panic . . . yet. Our spy would've alerted us if Amy and Dan had made any dangerous discoveries.

INFORMATION DISCOVERED

Clue: _____

My Notes on Rival Agents: _____
_____
_____
_____

Hints Gathered on Future Clue Locations: _____
_____
_____
_____

New Cahill Founder Identified: _____
_____
_____
_____

New Information Uncovered: _____
_____
_____
_____

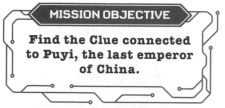

MISSION OBJECTIVE

Find the Clue connected to Puyi, the last emperor of China.

Agents Involved:

Amy and Dan Cahill (unknown)
Alistair Oh (Ekat)
Ian and Natalie Kabra (Lucian)
The Holts (Tomas)
Jonah Wizard (Janus)

Locations:

- **Beijing,** China
- **Xian,** China
- **Denfeng,** China
- **Final Location Unknown**

Challenges:

- Find a hint hidden in a royal fortress
- Avoid being crushed in a lollipop factory
- Spar with kung fu masters
- Fight an ancient warrior
- Survive a trip to the most treacherous spot on earth

Intelligence report:

Amy and Dan arrived in China, but then something went wrong. They had a heated argument in Tiananmen Square and Dan stormed off. (It's unclear what they were fighting about. We can only hope it had nothing to do with the information hidden in Grace's house in Madagascar.) We believe the children tried to meet back up, but it was too late. For the first time in their lives, Dan and Amy are apart—desperately trying to find each other in a country of over one billion people. Subsequently, their Clue hunt might end earlier than expected. Alone, the children are highly vulnerable; there have already been rumors of an attack on Dan. Even if they somehow make it to the rumored Clue location, it's unlikely that both siblings will return. Grace knew the danger of sending her grandchildren to such a perilous spot. She must have decided that the Clue was worth the risk . . . and the sacrifice.

INFORMATION DISCOVERED

Clue: _____

My Notes on Rival Agents: _____
_____
_____
_____

Hints Gathered on Future Clue Locations: _____
_____
_____
_____

New Cahill Founder Identified: _____
_____
_____
_____

New Information Uncovered: _____
_____
_____
_____

BOOK NINE

STORM WARNING

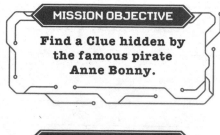

MISSION OBJECTIVE

Find a Clue hidden by
the famous pirate
Anne Bonny.

Agents Involved:

Amy and Dan Cahill (unknown)
Ian and Natalie Kabra (Lucian)

Locations:

- **Paradise Island,** Bahamas
- **Kingston,** Jamaica
- **Spanish Town,** Jamaica
- **Port Royal,** Jamaica

Secrets revealed:

- The real danger of the Clue hunt
- Nellie's hidden past
- The truth about the Madrigals
- The identity of the man in black

Intelligence report:

After surviving a trip to one of the most deadly
locations on earth, Amy and Dan followed a
lead to the Caribbean. En route, their suspicions
about their au pair, Nellie, caused them to
confront her. Nellie broke protocol and revealed
too much about her secret employer. She will be
dealt with accordingly. Amy and Dan discovered
that the Clue was related to a missing artifact
and tracked it to Jamaica, where they were at-
tacked by the Kabras. That's when the accident
occurred. We're still collecting information but,
unfortunately, it appears that the rumors might
be true. We're sending an agent to Jamaica
to conduct a full investigation, as we do for all
deaths on the hunt.

INFORMATION DISCOVERED

Clue: _____

My Notes on Rival Agents: _____
_____
_____
_____

Hints Gathered on Future Clue Locations: _____
_____
_____
_____

New Cahill Founder Identified: _____
_____
_____
_____

New Information Uncovered: _____
_____
_____
_____

BOOK TEN

CLASSIFIED

BOOK TEN

THE 39 CLUES

MISSION OBJECTIVE

ON A NEED TO
KNOW BASIS

Agents Involved:

NOT FOR
PRYING EYES

Locations:

FOR MADRIGAL
AGENTS ONLY

Secrets revealed:

TOO SECRET
TO REVEAL

Intelligence report:

SECRET

MY THEORIES

Clue? _____

My Guess at the Title: _____

_____

_____

_____

My Guess About Where They Go: _____

_____

_____

_____

New Cahill Founder Identified? _____

_____

_____

_____

New Information Uncovered? _____

_____

_____

_____

CARDS ARE YOUR KEY TO CLUES – COLLECT THEM ALL!

○ **1** Secret: Surveillance Camera •

○ **2** Agent: Dan Cahill •

○ **3** Secret: Catacombs •

○ **4** Secret: The Titanic •

○ **5** Agent: George McClain •

○ **6** Secret: Thomas Jefferson •

○ **7** Agent: Maria Marapao •

○ **8** Agent: Ophir Dhupam •

○ **9** Founder: Harry Houdini • •

○ **10** Founder: Flying Ace • •

○ **11** Location: Hidden Notes •

○ **12** Location: Taj Mahal •

○ **13** Secret: Frankenstein •

○ **14** Secret: Imposters • •

○ **15** Secret: Telegram •

○ **16** Secret: Eagle Eye • • •

○ **17** Secret: E-mail Code •

○ **18** Agent: Amy Cahill •

○ **19** Location: Monument Valley •

○ **20** Location: Racco Mansion •

○ **21** Agent: Lan Nguyen •

○ **22** Secret: Rocketboard •

○ **23** Agent: Victor Wood • •

○ **24** Agent: Lilya Chernova •

○ **25** Founder: Astronomer Royal • •

○ **26** Founder: Marie Curie •

○ **27** Location: Loch Ness •

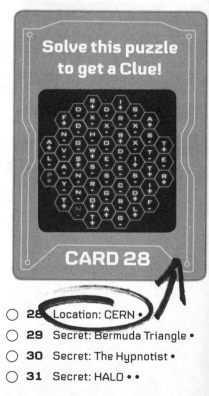

Solve this puzzle to get a Clue!

CARD 28

○ **28** Location: CERN •

○ **29** Secret: Bermuda Triangle •

○ **30** Secret: The Hypnotist •

○ **31** Secret: HALO • •

What does the man in the hat know about the death of Amy and Dan's parents?

CARD 96

**Find out what
Ian Kabra knows!**
CARD 178

**Discover Amy's
Madrigal Secrets!**

CARD 245

LEGEND

COMMON = •

UNCOMMON = • •

RARE = • • •

ULTRA-RARE = • • • •